Runaway Teacher

by

Pete Johnson

First published in 2000 in Great Britain by
Barrington Stoke Ltd
www.barringtonstoke.co.uk

This edition published 2007

Copyright © 2000 Pete Johnson

The moral right of the author has been asserted in
accordance with the Copyright, Designs and
Patents Act 1988

This book was inspired by the short story, 'CK Rules OK', published in *Secrets
from the Underground* in 1986

ISBN 978-1-84299-498-6

Printed in Great Britain by Bell & Bain Ltd

A Note from the Author

Real life is always interesting. There are ideas for stories in every street and every school. Wherever I go, my blue notebook goes too. Every day I'll write down things I see or overhear. (And yes, I am very nosy.)

Once I've got an idea, I nurse and coax it along. Then my imagination takes over. I start to picture characters and scenes in my mind. I become excited. Suddenly I can't get the story out of my head. I have to write it down.

And what's the end result? You're holding it in your hand.

Contents

Chapter 1
The Next Victim

It was the English lesson and we were waiting for our next victim. He was late.

"He's bottled out already," said my mate Martin Pepper, "because we're so frightening."

I laughed. No-one wanted to teach our English class. We'd already seen off two teachers this term. The last one just walked out. I can't really blame him. We'd nicked the keys to the stock room and locked him inside. He ran against the door like a mad bull. "Let me out," he screamed, over and over.

In the end we opened up. He stood and spluttered at us then marched away. We all cheered. But it was kind of shocking too.

"Here comes the new teacher," hissed Martin.

But actually it was Mr Morgan, the Headmaster. Everyone called him Moggie. He was very old and very scary. He glared at us. Then he pointed at me. He was always pointing at someone.

"Do we wear our uniforms like that, Scott Richards?" he barked at me. Before I could answer he said, "Do your top button up. Straighten up your tie. How many times have I told you about this?"

I did as I was told. I hoped I wasn't going bright red.

Then he gave us a lecture about how terrible we were. He said we were to treat our next teacher with respect. He went on at us a bit more and then he signalled to someone waiting outside.

The new teacher walked in, smiling. "Hi, everyone," he said.

Martin sniggered. "He won't last a week with us," he whispered.

"I'm pleased to introduce Mr Thompson," said the Headmaster. He gave us another warning glance and then he left.

Mr Thompson was surprisingly young for a teacher. He wore a trendy suit, a flashy tie and a big smile. "Now, I'd like everyone to call me Mark," he said. "I hate all this 'Sir' nonsense. It just gets in the way, doesn't it?"

We were immediately suspicious. We started to fire questions at him, just for the novelty of calling him Mark. Then we went back to calling him 'Sir'. It wasn't natural calling a teacher by his first name. It made him sound too human. Later we compromised and called him MT – his initials.

"Right," said MT, "I'm going to discover how talented you all are. I thought we'd start with a poem."

There were groans all around. "We can't do poetry," said Martin firmly.

"Rubbish," said MT. "Everyone can do poetry. I'm sure you've all written a poem that begins 'There was a ...' "

"You mean we can write poems like that!" exclaimed Martin.

"You can write anything you like," replied MT.

"Has it got to rhyme, Sir?" asked a girl at the front.

"No – and please don't call me Sir," said MT.

"How long has it got to be, Mark?" I asked, grinning as I said his name.

"As long as you like. Look, there are no rules, just write what you want – and enjoy yourself."

"You reckon," muttered Martin.

The girls in front of us were all whispering about MT ... Denise was saying the most.

"Fancy him, do you, Denise?" I asked.

She whirled round. "No," she snapped, "I just said he's quite fit for a teacher."

Martin turned to me, "Scott, let's give this guy some poems to remember."

So we wrote down really silly things. We read lines aloud and we both kept cracking up.

Denise heard us and turned round again. "You can't write that," she cried.

"Why not?" said Martin. "We were told to write anything we wanted."

"He'll send you to the Headmaster," said Denise.

"That's it," I cried. "I'll write a poem about old Moggie."

I set to work.

Martin read bits over my shoulder. "MT will go mad when he sees that," he said.

I agreed. It was pretty rude, actually.

I hesitated. "Perhaps I shouldn't hand it in to him."

But Martin had already snatched up the poem and given it to MT.

"I bet he doesn't come in smiling tomorrow," said Martin.

Chapter 2
My Mate MT

But the next day MT looked surprisingly cheerful.

"Thanks for all the poetry," he said.

"Enjoyed it, did you?" called out Martin.

"I certainly did," replied MT. "I won't say it's the best poetry I've ever read – but it shows promise. Let me show you what I mean. Here's one from Scott. It's called *The Headmaster*," said MT. Then he started reading.

Most of his day is over
his little light is out
What used to be his sex appeal
is now his waterspout
It used to be embarrassing
to make the thing behave
For nearly every morning it
stood up and watched him shave
But now he's on the downward slope
and can't see past his middle
And if he did he'd have a shock –
Now he can hardly raise a wiggle

He's being sarcastic, I thought. I'm going to get done for this. My heart started to thump.

Andy squeezed my knee. "Don't get embarrassed, Scott," he said, laughing.

The class clapped and whistled. And no-one clapped louder than MT. "Scott's poem was lively, funny and original," he said. Then he read several other poems aloud and seemed to be enjoying each one.

"Tell you what," he said. "I'd like to put all your poems in a book."

"Why?" I asked.

"Because I really like them." MT brought out this swish folder and some paper which looked expensive. Too good for my poem, in fact.

"I'd be really grateful if you'd copy out your poems on to this paper," he said. "Then I can keep them."

"He's gone mad," I muttered. But I took my poem home. I wanted to improve it. I spent half the night on it.

Soon I was doing a lot of work for English. MT never covered your work in red ink either. He just made what he called 'suggestions'.

MT was very helpful. He never minded explaining things again after the lesson. And in the lessons he seemed to be really enjoying himself. He was so relaxed. He'd lean right back in his chair. He'd have his shirt sleeves rolled up and his tie thrown right over his shoulder. Often he'd read a story aloud to us. And he'd use different voices for all the characters. I think he liked doing that.

He filled the classroom with his books too – mostly tatty old paperbacks. But he spoke so keenly about them he made you want to read them. I've still got the book he lent me, *The Catcher in the Rye*. I'll never be able to return it to him now.

Everyone said MT was a bit weird, but they liked him too. You never knew what he was going to do next.

Then one Saturday Martin and I saw MT in the town centre. He was coming out of the library. Under one arm was a pile of books. His other arm was round a girl. In fact she was just the kind of girl I like. MT and I clearly had a similar taste in women.

Now most teachers jump into a shop and hide if they spot a pupil. Not MT. He came over. And he introduced his girlfriend to us, just as if we were his mates. She was called Melanie and she was very pretty.

"Do you know he's been in that library for hours," moaned Melanie. "It's like his second home."

"Fancy a coffee?" asked MT.

Over coffee he told us that he and Melanie had met at university. They'd been going out together for nearly three years.

"Do you two live together?" I asked.

There was a silence.

"Or perhaps I shouldn't ask," I said.

"No, no," said Melanie. "It's just that this is something we've often discussed."

"Oh," I felt rather awkward.

"But at the moment," said MT firmly, "it's impossible. Melanie's a solicitor in London and as you know I'm teaching here."

"Get a job in London," suggested Martin.

"Thank you, Martin," said Melanie. "That's exactly what I say."

"So where do you live now?" I asked MT.

"Number 10 Blackwood Close. It's handy because it's near the school. I lodge with this old lady ..."

"Who washes his clothes and cooks his meals," interrupted Melanie.

"And lets me win at cards. I won 50p last night." MT seemed pleased about this.

"So you only see Melanie at weekends," said Martin. "I don't think I could bear that." He was flirting like mad now. But he will flirt with anyone, even my Mum.

Melanie played up to him. "Thank you, Martin. I'm glad someone appreciates me."

"Why don't you get yourself a proper job?" Martin asked MT.

"Teaching is a proper job," replied MT. "It's a genius way to spend your time. I'm very lucky."

"Lucky?" repeated Martin in amazement.

"Yes, because teachers can go on enjoying the teenage years over and over." He leaned forward. "Teachers can stay young all their lives."

"As you can see," said Melanie, "your teacher is just a big kid." She was smiling as she said it, at least I think she was.

It had been so good chatting with MT and meeting his girlfriend. And I really did look on MT as a mate.

And that's why what happened a couple of days later was so shocking.

Chapter 3
The Spy in the Class

It all started on Monday afternoon in the middle of our English lesson. This Year Seven boy came in and handed a note to MT. "The Headmaster says you must read this out right away," he said.

"Don't tell me the world is going to end in ten minutes," said MT. But the boy didn't smile.

After he'd gone MT shook his head. "No, this is very important indeed." He turned to us. "Ladies and gentlemen, I must ask you please to raise your feet in the air."

We gaped at him in astonishment.

"Why?" asked Martin.

"I'm not allowed to tell you yet. Just do it," said MT, gravely.

We were all greatly puzzled but we slowly leant back and held our feet up. There were some muffled giggles. But MT looked very serious as he walked up and down the rows.

Then he shook his head grimly. "Just as I suspected. You are not wearing grey socks as you should. Instead, you are wearing red and black socks and someone's even got white socks on. Why is that?"

No-one answered. All at once MT began to shake with laughter. "I'm sorry," he chuckled, "but have you ever heard of anything so daft. I mean, who cares what colour your socks are? Who cares?"

We all started to laugh too. We were totally amazed. All the other teachers moaned on and on about uniform.

"I've got some other important matters to check," continued MT. "Anyone wearing trainers is supposed to be sent to the Headmaster right away."

"That's not fair," cried Martin. "We shouldn't be told what shoes we can wear."

"I agree with you," said MT. "It's so patronising. You've got much more important things to worry about – like your exams. Well, I'm not sending anyone to the Headmaster for wearing trainers."

The whole class began to clap. MT smiled. "Girls," he said, "I'm supposed to study your jewellery and check that you're not wearing the wrong size earrings. There's a whole page of this rubbish. It's all so petty, isn't it?"

He shook his head. "I don't know, I've spent four years studying the world's greatest books. For what? To end up doing a sock check! Well, I'm not going to do it."

He went over to the bin. Then he tore old Moggie's note into tiny pieces.

This time the clapping just went on and on. Then Martin stood up. "Three cheers for MT. Hip, hip, hooray." We were cheering so loudly the room seemed to shake.

Suddenly the door opened. The Deputy Headmistress looked in. She peered around the classroom. "Oh, sorry," she said to MT, "I didn't know there was a teacher in here." Then she left again.

"That's me told off," said MT. "You're all enjoying yourselves too much. Something must be wrong."

"All the other teachers are so stuffy," I said. "But MT, you're totally different. It's amazing you manage to fit into the same staff room as them."

MT laughed really loudly after I'd said that. Then he said, "OK, everyone, settle down and get back to work."

At once the whole class did as he asked. But Denise turned round to Martin and me. "He shouldn't have torn that note up," she whispered.

"Why not?" I demanded.

"Because it's important," replied Denise. "My parents sent me here because they like the uniform ..."

But I wasn't really listening to her.

****

At the end of school the Headmaster suddenly jumped out at me. He gave me the shock of my life. "Are we wearing our shirts outside our jackets now?"

"No, Sir."

"Well, tuck it in then lad. I'm surprised your teacher let you leave the classroom half-dressed. Which lesson have you just had?" he demanded.

"English, with Mr Thompson, Sir," I said.

A look of suspicion crossed the Headmaster's face. I got the feeling that MT wasn't one of his favourite teachers.

"Did he read out my notice?" he asked.

"Oh yes, Sir," I answered.

"Are you sure?"

At that moment I spotted MT. He saw me too. He winked, then sped away. The Headmaster went on questioning me for ages. But I didn't give anything away.

****

Next day our first lesson was English. But MT was very late. This was unusual. He was normally dead on time. At last he appeared.

"Sorry to keep you waiting," he hissed. Then he banged his books down. For once MT wasn't smiling.

"I've just had a long discussion with the Headmaster." MT scowled at us. "It seems we have a spy in the class." Suddenly I realised that MT was staring right at me.

"Why are you looking at me?" I demanded.

MT's voice began to shake. "You can't trust anyone, can you?" he snapped.

I stared at him. I was stunned.

"Well, I hope you got some gold stars for reporting me," he sneered.

I was too shocked to know what to say. I knew I was turning bright red. There were mutterings all around me.

"You're quite happy for me to be good to you," said MT. "But in spite of it all, I'm still the enemy. You don't owe me any loyalty, do you?" There was sarcasm in his voice now. "So you tell the Headmaster about me tearing up his note."

All at once I found my voice. "No, I didn't," I protested.

"I saw you," cried MT.

"No, you never. You don't know what I said to him," I yelled.

"Don't lie," cried MT, wearily. Then he sighed heavily.

"I'm not lying," I said.

"Oh, be quiet," muttered MT. "Anyway, I got a right roasting thanks to you."

I'd had enough. I couldn't take any more. I sprang to my feet. "I'm not staying here a minute longer," I shouted.

"Yes you are," cried MT, "or I'll send you to the Headmaster. Sit down now!" he barked.

Suddenly he sounded just like a normal teacher. Martin started to say something. But then he saw this really stern look on MT's face. So he just muttered to me, "I know you never grassed MT up." Then he added, "Did you?"

I just gave him a foul look.

At the end of the lesson MT didn't hang behind as he usually did. He just marched off.

I went over to Denise. "It was you who told on MT, wasn't it?" I said.

She jumped in surprise. "No."

"Yes it was," I repeated.

"No, it was my Mum actually," she whispered. "I just happened to mention what Mr Thompson did and she thought it was disgraceful. She said if you're not going to wear uniform properly, there's no point in having it."

"Oh, who cares about school uniform," I snapped.

"My Mum does. She says if you look smart you work better. And it's part of MT's job to check our uniform." Denise lowered her voice even further. "Actually, I think she's right. MT tries too hard to be popular."

"No he doesn't," I cried. Then I wondered why I was defending him.

"He acts more like one of the pupils than a teacher," continued Denise. "And anyway, my Mum wasn't the only parent to ring up."

"What!"

"Two other parents rang up to complain as well," she said.

"Rubbish."

"I can't tell you their names but they did," Denise insisted. "I swear on my life."

Now that really shocked me. Everyone had cheered MT when he ripped that silly note up. Yet two other pupils had gone home and told their parents.

Martin, who was earwigging on our conversation said, "Go and see MT now. Clear your name."

"Why should I?" I said bitterly. "He's shown how much he trusts me. No, I've finished with him."

Chapter 4
A Teacher Apologises

That evening Martin and I sat on the fence by the crossroads. There was only one subject of conversation.

"MT's bang out of order," I said.

"That's true," agreed Martin.

"He saw me talking to the Headmaster and thought I was grassing him up. He never even gave me a chance to defend myself."

"I know," said Martin. "But MT was all worked up."

"That's no excuse," I replied.

"No, but I bet MT regrets what he said now," added Martin.

"Do you think so?" I asked.

"Oh, yeah," answered Martin. "Now he's had time to think about it, he'll know you didn't grass." He jumped down. "Why don't we go round to MT's house and talk to him about it," he suggested.

"No way."

"Go on," he urged.

"Well, we don't know where he lives," I said.

"Yes we do," Martin reminded me. "He told us. Remember? 10 Blackwood Close. He lives there with an old fossil."

"We can't just go round." I felt shy.

"Why not?" Martin demanded. "It could be a laugh. Besides, I've never been inside a teacher's house."

"He might not let us in," I said.

"I bet he does. He probably feels really bad about what happened."

35

"Well ..."

"Come on, mate," urged Martin. "We're not doing anything else."

We found MT's house easily. We knocked on the door. Someone drew back some curtains and unlocked the bolts. Then the door opened and a tottering, old lady peered out at us. This didn't quite go with MT's image.

"Is Mark in?" asked Martin.

"Yes," said the old lady. She looked at us both with suspicion.

"Can we see him?" asked Martin.

The old lady went on staring at us. I

don't think she was very impressed. "Who shall I say is calling?" she demanded.

"Two friends," said Martin.

She closed the door. She drew the curtains again too.

"I knew this was a bad idea," I muttered. I was getting more and more uneasy. I had a feeling MT would just tell us to clear off.

A few minutes later the door opened again. MT stood there. His shirt was hanging out and he looked as if he'd just woken up. He stared at us in amazement.

"Can we have a word?" asked Martin.

"Yes, sure, come through," he said.

I couldn't look at MT. I was angry with him, yet I felt dead embarrassed too.

We followed him into a drab-looking room. But the table was full of books, while in the centre of the room was this really expensive CD unit.

"Decent," muttered Martin, inspecting it.

"I bought that with my first pay cheque," said MT.

Martin started looking through MT's CD collection. "Hey, you've got some of the same CDs as me."

Martin sounded so amazed, MT laughed. And the atmosphere relaxed a bit.

Then I said, "We came round because you were mad at me this morning. I'm pretty angry too. Did you really think I'd tell on you to the Headmaster?" For the first time I looked directly at MT.

"I owe you a huge apology," said MT.

"Yes, you do," interrupted Martin. "Scott's been in a right sweat all day because of you."

"I feel really bad," said MT. "And afterwards when I thought about it properly ... I'm very sorry, Scott." It was strange having a teacher apologise to me. It had never happened before.

"That's OK," I muttered.

"Do you know who did ... sneak on me?" asked MT.

"Yes," I said. "It was Denise's Mum."

Martin looked uneasy. But telling MT wasn't like telling a normal teacher.

"I shan't do anything," said MT. "But thanks for letting me know the truth. And sorry again for accusing you, Scott. I just wasn't thinking properly today. You see, I got a nasty shock last night."

"What was that?" asked Martin at once.

Before MT could reply his landlady appeared again. "Help your guests to tea or coffee if you wish, Mark," she said.

"Thanks, Mrs Gable."

After she left MT asked, "Does anyone want coffee or tea?"

"What about something stronger?" asked Martin. He said it as a dare. He was always posing questions like that. He asked my Mum once if she wanted to play strip poker. But to my great amazement MT took Martin seriously.

"Well, I did have a little nip of whisky earlier," he confessed.

"And you know what they say about people who drink alone," teased Martin.

"Exactly," grinned MT. "Well, I'll get the whisky. Would you get the Coke out of the fridge? The kitchen's just through there." He pointed. Then he tore upstairs like a little kid who's been asked out to a party.

Martin flung open the fridge door. "See those pies. Do you think MT would mind if I heated one up?"

"Yes he would," I snapped. "We can't go eating all his food. Just bring the Coke like you were told."

"We're not at school now, you know," said Martin. Reluctantly he closed the fridge door. "I'm going to enjoy myself tonight," he added.

By now MT had sprinted downstairs with a large bottle of whisky. "Glasses, glasses," he said, all excited, as he dived into a battered, brown cupboard. Then he poured a small measure of whisky into three wine glasses – and picked up the Coke bottle.

"Say when," he said.

"Actually, MT, I prefer mine neat," said Martin.

I raised my eyes. That was a lie.

"A teacher is pouring me a drink," said Martin. "Now that's a strange event."

"Not really," replied MT. "Out of school I'm just like you."

"How old are you?" asked Martin.

"Guess," said MT.

"Forty," shouted Martin.

"Hey, hey," he cried.

"Fifty," I shouted.

"I'm six and a half years older than you, that's all," MT told them.

"Twenty two," said Martin. "Why, you're only two years older than my brother. I'd never have thought that."

"Well, cheers, Martin," he said.

"No, no," said Martin. "Actually, you do look young. You could be a sixth-former in fact."

We settled ourselves down on the hard chairs. "This is good," said MT, "sitting here with two mates. I feel better now."

"You never told us," I said hopefully, "about the nasty shock you got last night."

"Been chucked," said MT quickly. "Melanie rang me last night. She gave me the royal order of the boot." He smiled as he said it. But he wasn't really smiling.

I was shocked. They'd seemed so close when I saw them. I wasn't quite sure what to say.

Then Martin called out. "This is sad. Where's my hanky?" He began to sniff loudly.

Then suddenly he started laughing until I gave him a look. This was no laughing matter. It's awful being chucked. And I should know. I've been chucked twice in the last year.

"I'm really sorry," I said.

"Yes, it is bad," agreed Martin. "Still ..." he rubbed his face. "You'll meet someone else. You're not so old. There's this girl I like ..."

"Who we don't want to hear about now," I cut in.

Martin looked a bit hurt. "All right." Then he went on. "You haven't got anything to eat, have you MT? I'm starving."

"Yes, sorry. I'm being a very bad host." He leapt up. "How about a chocolate biscuit?"

"I was hoping for a sarnie, actually," replied Martin. "I was so worried about you and Scott that I hardly had any tea."

I made a scoffing noise. But MT said, "It's no problem making some sarnies. What would you like? Cheese, lettuce, tomato?"

"That'll be great," said Martin.

As soon as he'd gone into the kitchen Martin sprang up. He grabbed hold of the whisky bottle and poured a generous measure into his glass.

"Here, steady," I cried. Then Martin started gulping it down.

"What are you doing?" I asked.

"Enjoying myself," cried Martin, helping himself to another glass of whisky.

"Would anyone like tea or coffee now?" asked MT.

"Go on then," said Martin. "Make a pot of tea if you like." Then he called, "MT what goes in dry and comes out wet? A tea bag." Martin laughed at his silly joke. And MT laughed too in the kitchen.

Then Martin swallowed down yet another glass of whisky.

He was on his fourth glass when MT returned with a tray of tea and sandwiches. "Hope the tea's not too strong," he said.

Martin took one sip and said. "No, that's great." He grinned. "It's quite good having a teacher wait on us." He nibbled one of the sandwiches. Then he returned to his whisky.

I tried to get back to MT's problem. "Why did Melanie chuck you?" I asked quietly.

He considered for a moment. "She chucked me because ... she said she was tired of waiting for me to grow up. She wants to settle down, have a nice little house, children, all the trappings – and I just don't feel ready."

"Why not?" I asked.

"Good question." He started talking to me really honestly. It was fascinating. I'd never had such a deep chat with anyone before.

Suddenly I noticed that Martin had gone all quiet. I glanced at him. He was staring into space. I don't think he was listening to the conversation at all.

"It's good to talk to someone about all this," said MT.

I realised how lonely he was. I smiled at him. Then I looked at Martin again. He was swaying from side to side. And he had this glassy look on his face. He was really worrying me now.

"I've been bottling up things for a while," went on MT. "And I ..."

He was interrupted by Martin shouting out. "Oh no." We both gaped at him. Then Martin staggered to his feet. "MT, where's your loo?"

"Just past the kitchen. But are you all right?" exclaimed MT.

Martin didn't answer. Instead, he threw up on the carpet. Then he charged into the loo – for more of the same, no doubt.

"He's almost finished the bottle," I exclaimed.

But MT was looking at something else. A generous helping of puke glistening and glowing in the lamplight.

Chapter 5
Something On The Carpet

"Oh no," moaned MT. "My landlady will go mad when she sees this."

I nodded.

"I'd better clear it up," he said.

I nodded again.

MT hesitated. "How do you think I should do that?"

"You should get Martin to do it," I replied. "It's his fault."

"No, I'll do it," said MT. "I was just wondering how."

I considered. "Well, a mate of mine hoovered it up."

"Mmm, yes, why not," cried MT. "Now, where is the hoover? Oh yes, under the stairs." He opened his door. I could hear the TV blaring away in his landlady's room. She was watching it with two of her chums. This disguised the noise of MT easing the hoover out of the cupboard and back into his room. "Will you switch the telly on, Scott?" he asked.

I put it on the channel his landlady was watching. It was one of those quiz shows. One where the audience clap and cheer if the contestant gets his own name right.

Then MT switched on the hoover. The hoover didn't seem to like the lumps of puke it had to pick up. And the slushy noise the vomit made as it was sucked up turned my stomach.

A horrible, manky mess remained on the carpet. The smell made me want to heave.

"I'll have to try and soak it up," he said, and ran into the kitchen to get a cloth. He came back. "I'll buy her a new cloth tomorrow." Certainly, that cloth couldn't be used again.

"I'd better go and see what Martin's doing," I said. Although I could guess.

The loo door was locked.

"All right, Martin?" I called.

"Yeah, go away. I'll be out in a minute," he moaned.

I went back to MT's room. He was scrubbing the carpet while the audience on the quiz show was shouting and whistling.

"It still reeks in here," I muttered.

"I've got an idea," said MT.

He charged upstairs. Moments later he came down again clutching his cans of smellies. We both started to spray them around the room. We kept on until we began to cough.

"Have we hidden the sick smell?" he asked.

"I'd say we've replaced it with an even worse smell," I pointed out.

MT looked worried. "And there's still the stain," he said, sadly. "We can't seem to get rid of that."

"Tell you what," I suggested, "if we move that table over the stain your landlady won't notice it."

While we were heaving the table Martin reappeared. Tiny globules of sick hung on his lips. He looked terrible.

"Wipe your mouth, Martin," I said briskly.

He fell into a chair, shoved his sleeve over his mouth and muttered. "I want to go home."

"How far's he got to go?" asked MT.

"He lives a bit further away than me. So it's not far."

"I'll get you both a taxi," said MT.

But Martin stumbled to his feet and insisted, "I want to go home now."

"Do you still feel bad, Martin?" asked MT.

He nodded.

"I think he might be sick again," I whispered. "It's probably better if we shoot off now."

"Well, if you're sure," replied MT.

"I'll look after him," I said.

We propelled Martin towards the door.

"Smell's not too bad now, is it?" asked MT, anxiously.

I felt really sorry for him. "No, and anyway your landlady's old, and probably won't have a very good sense of smell."

Any further discussion was cut short by Martin throwing up on the next-door neighbour's wall.

"I'll get him home quick," I said. "And cheers for a good evening."

"Yes, it was a good evening, wasn't it?" He smiled. I only ever saw him smile once more.

Walking Martin home was very tiring and very boring. It was my bad luck that he hung on to me. My bad luck, because the smell Martin gave off was not a pleasant one. Also, he was gabbling on about a girl.

"She's so brilliant, dead pretty and with a great personality. I love her, you know – and she loves me too."

"Yeah, yeah, yeah," I replied. It was freezing cold and I just wanted to get home. "Come on, speed up."

"No, honestly Scott, I do," he whined. "And I want to tell her how much I love her. Let's go and find her."

He was doing my head in now. "Don't be stupid," I snapped. "You don't even know where she lives."

Martin wrenched himself free from me. "I'm not being stupid." He was getting worked up. "And I'm not the one who's been chucked twice."

"All right, all right," I muttered. "At least girls go out with me. They never go near you. And who can blame them?"

Now that was a bit nasty. Martin's not exactly good-looking – he's a lot shorter than me, as well as being overweight. Also, he tries too hard with the girls which always puts them off.

"Thanks, mate," he muttered.

Then, before I realised it he'd marched away. He was quivering with indignation.

"Where are you going?" I called.

"None of your business."

"Martin, look, I'm sorry," I began.

"Shut up," snapped Martin. "And you needn't come with me. In fact, I'd prefer it if you didn't."

I should have followed him. I meant to. But I thought he wasn't very far away from his house. And I was cold and very tired. And he was really getting on my nerves.

So I left Martin and went home. I fell asleep as soon as my head hit the pillow.

Next morning I was woken up by my Mum – and a policeman.

Chapter 6
Teachers Can't Run Away

The policeman stood over me. He was holding a notebook.

"This is a policeman," said my Mum, as if I didn't know. "He wants to ask you some questions." She sounded frightened.

"I would like you to tell me what you did last night," began the policeman.

"Well, I went out about seven o'clock with Martin Pepper and I got back about half past ten, maybe a bit later." I was trying to speak really calmly but I was terrified.

"Where had you been?" he asked.

"I just went to see someone," I replied.

"Who?"

"A friend. Well, not exactly a friend. A teacher," I said.

"What's his name?" demanded the policeman.

"Mr Thompson," I answered.

"Who lives at ..." Then he read out MT's address. I shivered. How did he know where MT lived already?

"What's happened?" I croaked.

The policeman didn't answer. Instead he asked, "Tell me, Scott, how much alcohol was consumed at Mr Thompson's?"

"What!" Just where was this leading?

He repeated the question.

"Not much," I said. "About half a glass. Why are you asking this?"

His tone grew harsh. "Because your friend Martin Pepper was found lying unconscious in a garden last night."

I started breathing really quickly, like someone who's been holding their breath for too long.

"And if the owner of the garden hadn't noticed Martin Pepper he'd probably have died of exposure by now," continued the policeman, glaring at me.

"And where is Martin ...?" I began.

"In hospital," he replied. "I spoke to him about half an hour ago. He's still in a very weak state and remembers very little of what happened last night. But I know he'd been drinking very heavily. So I want you to tell me what pubs you visited last night. I can check but I'd rather you told me."

The policeman loomed over my bed. My

Mum's eyes were boring into me. I was on trial in my own bedroom.

"We didn't go to any pubs," I said.

"Are you sure?" he asked.

I nodded. Later I wished I'd lied. But I was too confused to think properly.

"So Martin Pepper became extremely drunk because of what he'd consumed with Mr Thompson?" asked the policeman.

My Mum started making 'tut-tutting' noises.

"How much did your teacher offer Martin Pepper to drink?" The policeman wanted to know.

"Only one very small glass," I cried. "But Martin helped himself when Mr Thompson wasn't looking."

But PC Plod wasn't buying that. Instead he lowered his voice. "Scott, are you in the habit of going round to teachers' houses?"

"No."

"Yet this teacher invited you two around to his house and offers you unlimited drink ... tell me, has this teacher been showing you any special attention?"

I knew which way his mind was working. I began to get angry. "Actually, we were giving him advice because he'd just split up with his girlfriend," I said.

"And why does that concern you?" The policeman's voice was all soft and creepy. He was determined to find something sinister in all this.

"Why shouldn't he discuss his problems with us?" I retorted. "He's a young teacher and he hasn't got many mates ..."

"Really," said the policeman, raising an eyebrow. He was scribbling down everything I said.

As soon as he'd gone, I had a second cross-examination from my Mum. "Why did you go round to his house? Does he live alone? Why did he give you all that drink?"

I couldn't explain it to her. And when I said, "Poor MT," she exclaimed, "Poor

Martin, you mean. He's the one in hospital thanks to your teacher's irresponsible behaviour!"

"Mum, how many more times?" I protested. "Martin behaved like a kid and ruined our evening. It's all his fault."

"Your teacher was in charge of you," my Mum retorted. "He should have stopped Martin. I'm really shocked you were drinking. You know what your father thinks about that."

My Dad never touches drink. He thinks it causes many of today's problems. He gets really wound up about it.

"I suppose the teacher forced that drink on you," prompted my Mum.

It saved time to agree. And it meant my Dad wouldn't be so mad at me. So I mumbled. "Well, he was feeling a bit lonely ..."

"He ought to be struck off, that teacher of yours," my Mum went on. "He's a disgrace. An absolute disgrace."

I felt awful afterwards, as if I'd betrayed MT. But I didn't want to get in my Dad's bad books either. For when he gets mad at you, he stays mad for days afterwards.

As soon as I got to school I looked for MT. He never went to the staff room. He was absent all day. And I don't think he'd phoned in because no-one was covering his classes.

After school I went round to his digs. His landlady didn't look very pleased to see me again.

"Hello, is Mark there please?" I asked.

"No, he isn't. He's probably still at school."

But I knew he wasn't there.

"I had the police round here, first thing this morning." She stared angrily at me. "Were you the boy who was sick all over my carpet?"

So she'd noticed. "No, that wasn't me," I said quickly and left.

Later I went to see Martin in hospital. My Mum gave me the bus fare and a box of chocolates. But I had to promise to come straight back as my Dad wanted to talk to me. Another telling off, I thought gloomily.

Martin was lying in bed grinning all over his face. "It's a great laugh in here. And the nurses are gorgeous. There's one who really fancies me. She keeps giving me the eye."

I was relieved to see Martin was all right. Yet I also felt cross that he was looking so happy.

"Are those chocolates for me?" he asked.

"My Mum bought them, not me," I said shortly.

"Tell your Mum she's gorgeous too," cried Martin. "And have a chocolate. Only don't take a caramel one as they're my favourites."

I frowned at him.

"So what happened to you last night?" I asked.

"It's all a blank," he said. He was enjoying the drama.

"Oh yeah," I said. "You've caused a right mess, you have. I've had the police round my house, my Mum's gone up the wall and when I go back I've got my Dad to face."

Martin grinned uneasily.

"MT's in big trouble because of you," I continued.

Martin shrugged. "So what? He's only a teacher."

That got me really angry. I picked up Martin's box of chocolates and punched it hard. The chocolates flew everywhere. "He wasn't only a teacher, he was our mate," I cried. "And we've just ruined his entire career."

Then I stormed out.

Martin shouted after me. "Bet you wish you'd seen me home, don't you, Scott?"

I wished a lot of things. But mainly I wished I could talk to MT. I went back to his house. His landlady answered again. She told me he hadn't come home yet.

It was nearly seven o'clock. Wherever could he be? I was getting really worried now. Then, suddenly, an idea hit me. And I thought, I know where MT has gone.

Chapter 7
A Gift from MT

I went to the town library. Hadn't Melanie said this was MT's second home?

It was surprisingly busy and at first I couldn't see MT. But then I spotted him, right at the end of the library. He didn't see me. He was lost in the book he was reading.

I rushed over to him. "Hi," I said. He nearly dropped the book with surprise.

"Hello, Scott," he replied.

Then I felt suddenly awkward. I wasn't sure what to say next.

"What are you reading?" I asked.

"*War of the Worlds* by H.G. Wells," he replied.

"Oh, I've heard of that," I said.

"Yes, it's a brilliant story, really exciting too," said MT. "I've got an old copy at my landlady's. But I felt like reading a bit now."

Then he started telling me the story. It was all about these Martians. He got really keen.

"You've made me want to read it right now," I told him.

"You can borrow my copy," he said eagerly.

"Thanks!" Then I went on. "Look, I'm really sorry about last night."

"No, it was my fault," he replied. "How's Martin?"

"He's never had it so good," I said, bitterly. "No, he's great." I looked at him. "You treated us like mates last night. And we let you down."

"Perhaps I had no business treating you as mates," replied MT. "That's what the policeman said to me. He also said they're going to throw the book at me. Apparently I'm a very bad influence."

I sat down opposite him then said quietly, "You weren't at school today."

"No." He looked away just as if I were the teacher, not him. "I couldn't face it. So I ran away."

"Teachers can't run away," I said.

"Believe me, they can," he replied.

"I bet you've been in here all day, haven't you?" I asked.

He nodded.

"But you've got to go back," I said, quietly.

"Yes, I know." His voice was even quieter than mine.

I looked at my watch. It was nearly eight o'clock. "I'm going to have to go," I said. "Or my parents will kill me."

"Yes, of course," replied MT. "Thanks for looking for me. And don't worry, Scott, I'll be back at school tomorrow."

"Excellent." I got up. Then I added, "When you go home you might want to give Melanie a bell."

Then I rushed off home.

Next morning I was at school really early. I thought MT might need a bit of moral support. I walked into his classroom – and got the shock of my life.

MT was there but he was packing up all his things.

"What are you doing?" I cried.

He turned and faced me. "I've already seen the Headmaster who knows about ... everything. He said I've been immature and stupid and brought disgrace on the school."

"Oh no," I muttered.

"Actually, I think he was just looking for an excuse to sack me," said MT. "Although I haven't been sacked – they've let me resign."

"That's terrible." I exclaimed. "What will you do?"

"Oh, I had a feeling this might happen," he replied. "And last night ... well I took your advice and rang Melanie. She's got a friend in advertising who might be able to help."

"Are you two back together?" I asked.

"Let's say we're talking," he answered. "By the way, this is a little gift for you."

He threw a book at me. It was his copy of *War of the Worlds*.

"Sorry it's a bit worn," he said.

"No, I'll look after it," I replied. "I'll read it too. I promise."

"That's good to hear." Suddenly MT's face broke into a wide smile.

"It'll be funny coming in here and not seeing you," I said. "I bet we get a real gormo in your place too."

"Well," said MT, "I'm going to miss chilling out with you lot – and talking about books and stuff. It was all the other things I wasn't prepared for ..." Then he picked up his bag and said, "I want to slip away before the rest of the class arrive."

I walked with him to his car.

Then I extended my hand to him. We shook hands.

"Why are we shaking hands?" he asked.

My voice started to shake. "Don't know exactly," I mumbled. "I just wanted to say ... well I think you're a good teacher and I won't forget you."

He didn't answer. He just gave me a quick wave and drove away really fast. But I think there were tears in his eyes.

I never saw MT again.

The publishers would like to thank the
Royal High School, Edinburgh, for
all their help – in particular Dylan Bartlett,
Lochie Brown and Mark Macauley who
volunteered to appear on the front cover

Barrington Stoke would like to thank all its readers for commenting on the manuscript before publication and in particular:

Chris Baines
Grace Chalcott
Jonathan Donegan
Sophie Green
Stephanie Hallin
Sam Hughes
Emily Lestor
Alex McRae-Ironside
Margaret Morris
Seth Munn
Steven Nairn
Sonia Robertson
Evelyn Smith
Danie Thorpe-Tracy
Staci Turner

Become a Consultant!

Would you like to give us feedback on our titles before they are published? Contact us at the email address below – we'd love to hear from you!

info@barringtonstoke.co.uk
www.barringtonstoke.co.uk

If you loved this book, why don't you read ...

Diary of an (Un)teenager

by Pete Johnson

ISBN 1-842991-94-9

Sunday, June 21st

"... I won't have anything to do with designer clothes, or girls, or body piercing, or any of it ... no, I shall let it all pass me by. Do you know what I'm going to be? An (Un)teenager.

But then Spencer's best mate Zac starts wearing baggy trousers and huge trainers – and even starts going on dates with girls. But Spencer is determined:
"Dear diary, I am going to stay EXACTLY as I am now. That's a promise ..."

A hilarious comedy by the "devastatingly funny Pete Johnson". *Sunday Times*

You can order *Diary of an (Un)teenager* directly from our website at **www.barringtonstoke.co.uk**